TWO
AUGHABLE LYRICS
by Mr. Edward Lear

e Pobble Who Has No Foes   *The Quangle Wangle's Hat*

Paul Galdone drew the pictures

G. P. PUTNAM'S SONS

New York

ABOUT THE BOOK

Of the many poems in the Lear canon, few are more beloved than The Pobble Who Has No Toes and The Quangle Wangle's Hat. In Two Laughable Lyrics, Paul Galdone once again complements Edward Lear's poetry in drawings that capture the flavor of Lear's own Victorian England and the whimsy of his verse.

Illustrations © 1966 by Paul Galdone
All rights reserved
Library of Congress Catalog Card Number: 66-14329
MANUFACTURED IN THE UNITED STATES OF AMERICA
Published simultaneously in the Dominion
of Canada by Longmans Canada, Limited,
Toronto
05208
Second Impression

THE POBBLE WHO HAS NO TOES

THE Pobble who has no toes
    Had once as many as we;
When they said, "Some day you may lose them all,"
    He replied, "Fish fiddle de-dee!"

And his Aunt Jobiska made him drink
Lavender water tinged with pink;
For she said, "The World in general knows
There's nothing so good for a Pobble's toes!"

The Pobble who has no toes
    Swam across the Bristol Channel;
But before he set out he wrapped his nose
    In a piece of scarlet flannel.

For his Aunt Jobiska said, "No harm
Can come to his toes if his nose is warm;
And it's perfectly known that a Pobble's toes
Are safe — provided he minds his nose."

The Pobble swam fast and well,
    And when boats or ships came near him,
He tinkledy-binkledy-winkled a bell
    So that all the world could hear him.

And all the Sailors and Admirals cried,
When they saw him nearing the further side,
"He has gone to fish, for his Aunt Jobiska's
Runcible Cat with crimson whiskers!"

But before he touched the shore —
  The shore of the Bristol Channel —
A sea-green Porpoise carried away
  His wrapper of scarlet flannel.

And when he came to observe his feet,
Formerly garnished with toes so neat,
His face at once became forlorn
On perceiving that all his toes were gone!

And nobody ever knew,
    From that dark day to the present,
Whoso had taken the Pobble's toes,
    In a manner so far from pleasant.

Whether the shrimps or crawfish gray,
Or crafty Mermaids stole them away,
Nobody knew; and nobody knows
How the Pobble was robbed of his twice five toes!

The Pobble who has no toes
  Was placed in a friendly Bark,
And they rowed him back, and carried him up
  To his Aunt Jobiska's Park.

And she made him a feast, at his earnest wish,
Of eggs and buttercups fried with fish;

And she said, "It's a fact the whole world knows,
That Pobbles are happier without their toes."

START FROM THE OTHER END ➤ NOW PLEASE TURN THIS BOOK OVER AND

And the Quangle Wangle said
    To himself on the Crumpetty Tree,
"When all these creatures move
    What a wonderful noise there'll be!"
And at night by the light of the Mulberry moon
They danced to the Flute of the Blue Baboon,
On the broad green leaves of the Crumpetty Tree,
And all were as happy as happy could be,
    With the Quangle Wangle Quee.

And the Attery Squash, and the Bisky Bat
All came and built on the lovely Hat
    Of the Quangle Wangle Quee.

And the Blue Baboon, who played the flute,
And the Orient Calf from the Land of Tute,

And the Dong with a luminous nose.

And the Golden Grouse came there,
And the Pobble who has no toes,
And the small Olympian bear,

And all of them said,"We humbly beg,
We may build our homes on your lovely Hat —
Mr. Quangle Wangle, grant us that!
Mr. Quangle Wangle Quee!"

The Snail and the Bumble-Bee,
   The Frog, and the Fimble Fowl
(The Fimble Fowl, with a Corkscrew leg);

And besides, to the Crumpetty Tree
Came the Stork, the Duck, and the Owl,

But there came to the Crumpetty Tree,
  Mr. and Mrs. Canary;
And they said, "Did ever you see
  Any spot so charmingly airy?
May we build a nest on your lovely Hat?
Mr. Quangle Wangle, grant us that!
O please let us come and build a nest
Of whatever material suits you best,
  Mr. Quangle Wangle Quee!"

The Quangle Wangle said
   To himself on the Crumpetty Tree,
"Jam, and jelly, and bread,
   Are the best of food for me!
But the longer I live on this Crumpetty Tree,
The plainer than ever it seems to me
That very few people come this way,
And that life on the whole is far from gay!"
   Said the Quangle Wangle Quee.

ON the top of the Crumpetty Tree
  The Quangle Wangle sat,
But his face you could not see,
  On account of his Beaver Hat.
For his Hat was a hundred and two feet wide,
With ribbons and bibbons on every side
And bells, and buttons, and loops, and lace,
So that nobody ever could see the face
  Of the Quangle Wangle Quee.

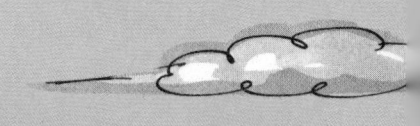

THE QUANGLE WANGLE'S HAT

EDWARD LEAR was the famous artist and humorist of the nineteenth century. Born in London in 1812, he began his career as an artist in the employment of the Earl of Derby, for whose son he composed the first BOOK OF NONSENSE. In the course of his career as a writer and illustrator, Lear traveled extensively throughout the European Continent, the Middle East, and India, turning out delightful travel memoirs and many books of humorous verse. John Ruskin placed the BOOK OF NONSENSE first in his list of a hundred delectable volumes of contemporary literature.

PAUL GALDONE was born in Budapest, Hungary, but he has lived in the United States since he was fourteen. Mr. Galdone studied at the Art Students League of New York and has illustrated many books for children. He has a special fondness for illustrating the poems of Edward Lear.

TWO
AUGHABLE LYRICS

by Mr. Edward Lear

e Quangle Wangle's Hat   The Pobble Who Has No Foes

Paul Galdone drew the pictures

G. P. PUTNAM'S SONS

New York